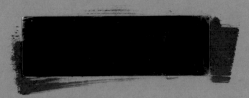

Creativity

Creativity

by John Steptoe / illustrations by E. B. Lewis

Clarion Books / New York

Clarion Books
a Houghton Mifflin Company imprint
215 Park Avenue South, New York, NY 10003
Text copyright © 1997 by The John Steptoe Literary Trust
Illustrations copyright © 1997 by E. B. Lewis

The illustrations for this book were executed in watercolor
on Arches 300-lb watercolor paper.
Text is 15/19-point Columbus.

Printed in the USA

Library of Congress Cataloging-in-Publication Data

Steptoe, John, 1950-1989
Creativity / by John Steptoe ; illustrations by E. B. Lewis.
p.   cm.
Summary: Charles helps Hector, a student who has just moved
from Puerto Rico, adjust to his new life.
ISBN 0-395-68706-3
1. Puerto Ricans—United States—Juvenile fiction.   [1. Puerto Ricans—
United States—Fiction.   2. Afro-Americans—Fiction.]
I. Lewis, E. B. (Earl B.), ill.   II. Title.
PZ7.S8367Cr 1997
[Fic]—dc20   96-34382
CIP
AC

HOR   10 9 8 7 6 5 4 3 2 1

To the children of Penn Wood Elementary
—*E. B. L.*

6

I was sittin' in class one day when this new dude walks in. He went over to Mr. Cohen's desk. Mr. Cohen's all right. He's my teacher.

Mr. Cohen stood up and said the new kid was named Hector. Hector's whole name was one of them long numbers. I'd get out of breath just tryin' to say it.

"Hector's family just moved here," Mr. Cohen said. "He'll be in our class. His two sisters will be going to school here too. I hope everyone will look out for Hector until he learns the ropes."

Then Hector said something to Mr. Cohen and Mr. Cohen said something back.

"What language you talkin', Mr. Cohen?" I asked.

"Spanish, Charles. Hector's from Puerto Rico," Mr. Cohen told me.

I didn't get it. How could that guy be from Puerto Rico? He was the same color as me, and I'm not from Puerto Rico. His hair was black like mine, but it was straight.

At the end of the day Mr. Cohen asked us, "Does anybody live near 66 Bergen Street? Hector and his sisters might need someone to make sure they don't get lost on the way home."

I raised my hand. "I'll walk 'em," I said. "I live right around the corner from there."

I went up to the front of the room and Mr. Cohen said, "Hector, this is Charles. He's going to walk home with you. Okay?"

Hector nodded and said, "Okay."

"Mr. Cohen, he can talk English," I said.

"Hector, you go ahead and meet the girls," Mr. Cohen said. "Charles will be right down."

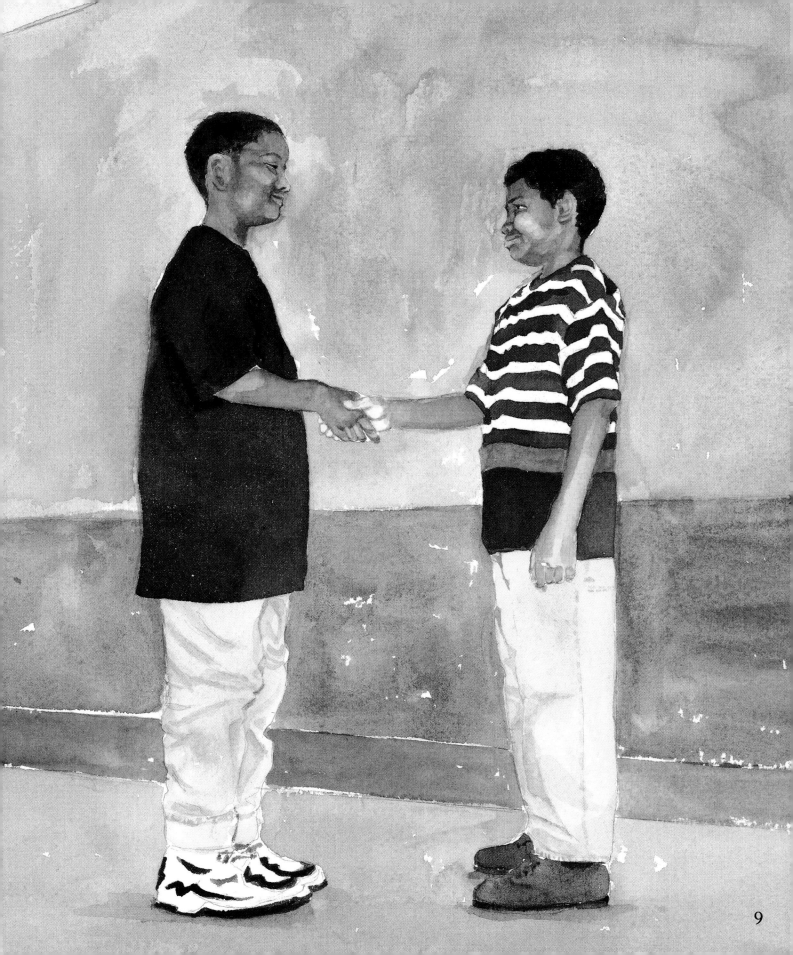

After Hector left, I said, "He ain't really Spanish, is he?"

Mr. Cohen laughed and said, "Hector isn't Spanish, but he speaks Spanish. People in the United States speak English, even though we're not all English."

"How come he's the same color I am? Don't that mean his people was from Africa like mine?"

"Charlie, the reason Hector looks so much like you is that his ancestry is similar to yours."

"You mean Hector's people was Africans too?"

"Yes."

I remembered that Hector's hair was straight.

"Africans and what else?"

"Africans and Spaniards from Spain and the Indians who originally lived on the island of Puerto Rico."

"They have Indians there?"

"That's right. Maybe tomorrow we can look at some maps and get into it a little more. But right now you should go downstairs and meet Hector and his sisters."

Hector was waiting with two girls. He told me the little one was Elsie and the bigger one was Rosita.

"What's happenin', sisters?" I said.

They both said, "*Buenos dias.*"

We started walkin'. Them girls was talkin' a mile a minute in Spanish. Boy! I didn't know how they could even understand themselves.

Hector and I walked behind them. Hector started tellin' me about his home in Puerto Rico. It wasn't easy to understand him at first, but I listened real hard. Hector is a nice dude, I thought.

13

When I got home I was tellin' my mother about Hector.

"I didn't know there were Puerto Ricans that looked just like us," I said.

"Yes, they come from pretty much the same type of people we come from," said Mamma. "Your father has some Cuban blood in him, and Cuba isn't far from Puerto Rico."

"Yeah?" I never knew I was part Cuban. "You know, Hector was tellin' me that his father was a fisherman in Puerto Rico. He used to help his father go fishin' sometimes. I didn't know people did things like that anymore. I thought they had machines to catch fish." Mama was smilin'. "Hector says they used to live on a beach with palm trees and coconut trees and stuff. Shoot, I wish I lived on a beach so I could go swimmin' every day."

"You better learn how to swim first," Mamma said.

"Hector says he can swim real good. Maybe he could teach me."

"Maybe," said Mamma.

Later when we was havin' dinner I was tellin' my father about Hector and swimmin' lessons.

"I was thinkin' I could trade teachin' him how to speak good English," I said.

Mamma laughed. "And who's gonna teach *you?*"

Daddy smiled and said, "Charlie's just bein' creative with his language. Right, Charles?"

Mamma and Daddy laughed. I laughed too, but I didn't know what we was laughin' at.

"What's *creative*, Daddy?"

"That's like when a musician takes a song and does something different with it—different from what anybody else does. Or when three painters sit in front of the same bowl of fruit and come up with three different pictures. Each of them has something different to say about that bowl of fruit, so each paints it in a different way. Understand?"

"Sort of."

Daddy thought for a minute. "Most of the people you know speak English, and you speak English too, right?"

"Yeah."

"Well, you speak it differently than anybody else. People can still understand you, but you're almost speaking a whole other language. You take the basic language and use it to express yourself the way you want to. Sayin' what you mean in your own special way—that's bein' creative."

"That's cool," I said. I liked knowin' there was a nice word for doin' things my own way. Hector had told me they don't speak Spanish in Puerto Rico the same way they speak it in Spain. I guess Puerto Ricans are bein' creative too.

The next day in school Mr. Cohen showed us Puerto Rico on a map. He was tellin' us that when the Spaniards came there they brought Africans as slaves to do the hard work, the way the English made slaves out of people that I probably came from and brought them to the United States. And then about how the Spanish people who came to the islands and the Africans and the Indians that already lived there and some Chinese people had all mixed together to make Puerto Ricans. Just like here, when some of the Africans mixed with some of the white people and I guess some Indians too.

"I guess if everybody don't kill each other everybody will get all mixed up together," I said. "That would be weird."

"Not so weird, when you think about it," Mr. Cohen said. "Everybody in this room is the result of different people mixing up together."

Our next class was gym. Me and Hector was talkin' while we were changin' into our gym clothes. Then Hector pulled out these brand new sneakers.

In this neighborhood you got to have the right sneakers 'less you want to get laughed at. I didn't want to hurt Hector's feelings, so I didn't say nothin' about them float-boats he was carryin' around on his feet.

21

When we got out on the gym floor, all the fellas was doin' a lot of laughin' and crackin' on Hector's sneakers.

"Hey, Hector, where'd you get them skips?"

"Charlie, you should refer your boy to a better store."

Hector got mad. "What's the big joke?" he asked me.

"Aw, they just actin' stupid," I said. "'Cause you dress different."

"What do you mean?"

23

"Well, your sneakers. And that shirt."

He looked down at the palm tree shirt.

"My grandmother gave me this shirt," he said. "I really like it. It reminds me of back home. And what's wrong with my sneakers?"

"Well, people around here are really into sneakers. And nobody wears that kind."

"My mother just bought them," Hector said. "They're brand new. She doesn't have money to buy me another pair."

"Don't worry about it," I said. "You still my boy even if you do dress weird."

When I got home I checked out my closet. My mother came into the room while I was lookin'.

"Charlie, what you doin'?"

"I'm lookin' for my other sneakers."

"You've got sneakers on your feet. How many pairs can you wear?"

"They not for me, they for Hector," I explained. "He didn't know the right kind to buy, and his mother can't get him no more 'cause she already bought him some. And I can't have none of my friends walkin' around lookin' funny if they gonna hang out with me."

"Well, I guess they're your sneakers," Mamma said.

The next day was Saturday. I took the sneakers and went over to Hector's house. Rosita answered the door.

"*Buenos dias*," I said.

She showed me where Hector's room was, doin' a lot of gigglin'. I went in.

"What's happenin', my man?"

"Hey, Charlie!" Hector jumped up. "How do you feel? Who opened the door for you?"

"Rosita."

"I think my sister likes you." Hector was grinnin'.

"Yeah?"

"Yeah, she always talkin' about you. What you got there in that box?"

"I got you a pair of sneakers. Good ones."

"For me?" He took the box and opened it. "Oh. Nice. They cost a lot of money?"

"No big thing. Put 'em on."

Hector sat down and started puttin' them on.

"I figured you wore the same size as me," I told him.

"Yes, they fit good." He stood up and bounced a little.

"Let's go play some ball," I said. "Try 'em out."

"Okay," Hector said. Then he said, "Wait a minute."

He went to his closet and pulled something out and handed it to me.

"Here." It was his palm tree shirt.

"You gonna give me your shirt? You don't have to do that," I said.

"It's a good exchange," Hector said.

I put on the shirt and looked at myself in the mirror. It looked great. And suddenly I knew exactly what to say.

"Your gift to me is very creative, Hector," I said. "I like it."
Then we went out to play ball.